THE GLASS MENORAH

THE GLASS MENORAH

and Other Stories for Jewish Holidays

Maida Silverman

ILLUSTRATED BY *Marge Levine*

FOUR WINDS PRESS ⟩W⟨ NEW YORK

Maxwell Macmillan Canada Toronto *Maxwell Macmillan International*
New York Oxford Singapore Sydney

In loving memory of Edith Friedman Silverman
and my parents and grandparents

—M.S.

To my mother and in loving memory
of my father

—M.L.

The author wishes to thank Judy Muffs, consultant, the Anti-Defamation League of B'nai B'rith, for her assistance. Text copyright © 1992 by Maida Silverman. Illustrations copyright © 1992 by Marge Levine. All rights reserved. No part of this book may be reproduced or transmitted in any form or by any means, electronic or mechanical, including photocopying, recording, or by any information storage and retrieval system, without permission in writing from the Publisher. Four Winds Press, Macmillan Publishing Company, 866 Third Avenue, New York, NY 10022. Maxwell Macmillan Canada, Inc., 1200 Eglinton Avenue East, Suite 200, Don Mills, Ontario M3C 3N1. Macmillan Publishing Company is part of the Maxwell Communication Group of Companies. First edition. Printed and bound in the United States of America   10 9 8 7 6 5 4 3 2 1   The text of this book is set in Cheltenham. The illustrations are rendered in watercolor, colored pencil, and pen and ink.

Library of Congress Cataloging-in-Publication Data   Silverman, Maida.   The glass menorah and other stories for Jewish holidays — Maida Silverman. — 1st American ed. p.   cm.   Summary: Eight stories, describing the way the Berg family celebrates various Jewish holidays, including the Sabbath, Rosh Hashanah, Simchat Torah, and Hanukkah.   ISBN 0-02-782682-1   1. Fasts and feast—Judaism—Juvenile fiction. 2. Children's stories, American. [1. Fasts and feast—Judaism—Fiction. 2. Family life— Fiction. 3. Jews—Fiction. 4. Short stories.] I. Title.   PZ7.S5863G1 1992   [Fic]— dc20   91-13890

Contents

TRADITIONS

A Story for the Sabbath

"It's very mysterious," said Mom, shaking a box filled with small squiggles of plastic foam. "I'm sure I packed both candlesticks together, but I can only find one!"

The Berg family had moved into their new house on Thursday. Today was Friday, Sabbath would begin at sunset, and everything was still topsy-turvy. Mom, Dad, Abby, Ben, and Molly were all searching among the packing boxes for the special things they needed to welcome the first Sabbath in their new home.

"I found the Sabbath wine decanter," said Dad, holding up a pretty glass bottle. "But I can't find the kiddush cup."

"I can't find the challah bread tray," said Abby, who was ten and the oldest. Suddenly a loud thud came from the kitchen, where Ben and Molly were. The others hurried toward the noise.

"Molly and I were trying to open this," said Ben, pointing to a large box lying on its side. "It sort of fell over." Ben was going on nine.

His father turned the box right side up and read the label.

"Pots and pans are in here. No harm done," he said cheerfully.

Thump! Bump! Clatter!

"*Now* what?" cried Dad. Everyone ran into the living room.

Bessie, the cat, had climbed into a box on the sofa. The box had tipped over, spilling spoons, forks, and Bessie onto the floor.

Mom removed a pile of books and a teapot from a nearby chair and sat down. "I know everyone wants to help," she said. "But we'll do better with fewer helpers. Max, I'd like you and Molly to go to town to buy Sabbath candles. Ben and Abby, please stay and help unpack."

Six-year-old Molly was glad for the chance to see the new town. She got into the car with her father. They backed out of the driveway and turned right, then left.

They drove for quite a while along a road with trees and fields on both sides. Dad began to look more and more puzzled. Finally he stopped the car by the side of the road.

"I think we're lost," he said.

Molly looked around and saw another parked car. "Look!" she said, pointing. "There's someone we can ask."

Almost hidden by a large clump of goldenrod was an elfin-looking elderly man, picking flowers.

"You aren't lost," he told them cheerfully when Dad asked for directions. "The town is just a bit farther down the road."

The sun had almost set by the time Dad and Molly arrived home with the candles. Sabbath would begin soon. They hurried up the walk, and Dad opened the door.

"Wow!" Molly said.

In the middle of the clutter of boxes and cartons stood the dining room table, all set and ready for the Sabbath. Mom had found a pretty tablecloth—it didn't matter that it was a bit wrinkled—and she'd spread it on the table. Challah rested in the challah tray. Abby had found it, after all. The wine decanter stood at Dad's place—and so did the kiddush cup.

"I found the missing candlestick," said Mom happily.

Tap, tap, tap! Someone was knocking gently at the door. Standing on the step was the elfin-looking man, holding a large bunch of flowers.

"Please come in," said Abby.

"My name is Mr. Yomtov," the man told them. "I live a few doors away, and I saw you move in." He held out his bouquet.

"It's a tradition to have fresh flowers on the table for the Sabbath, so I picked some of my favorite wildflowers for you, to wish you all a good Sabbath in your new home." He winked at Molly. "Some of your family I have already met."

Dad explained how he and Molly had met Mr. Yomtov.

"Thank you for the lovely flowers," said Mom. "Please stay for supper and share the Sabbath with us. That's a tradition, too."

"I would be honored and delighted to stay," said Mr. Yomtov.

Ben added a place at the table for Mr. Yomtov. Abby put the flowers into a vase of water and set it on the table. Mom lit the candles in the tall candlesticks and recited the blessing that welcomed the Sabbath.

The worry and scurry of the topsy-turvy day vanished. In their place was Sabbath peace and joy. Even Bessie seemed to know the Sabbath had come. She sat quietly in a chair, the candlelight shining in her golden eyes.

Dad held up the kiddush cup. He said the blessing for wine and passed the cup for all to sip and share the blessing. He cut a slice of challah and said the blessing thanking God for bread. Then he gave some challah to each person to eat, to share in that blessing, too.

"Good Sabbath!" said Mr. Yomtov, looking around at the smiling faces. "God bless this house!" And everyone said, "Amen!"

A SKIPJACK AND A FRESH START

A Story for Rosh Hashanah

"**B**en," called Molly. "Please come take this pesky cat. She keeps jumping onto the table and getting in our way!"

It was a few days before Rosh Hashanah. Molly and Abby were sitting at the kitchen table, getting ready to send New Year cards. They were writing *"L'shana tova tikatevu"*—"May you have a happy year"—inside each one.

Ben came into the kitchen and scooped Bessie up in his arms.

"Is your dumb friend Debbie really spending the holidays with us?" he asked Abby.

"She's coming tomorrow," Abby told him. "And she isn't dumb."

"Mr. Yomtov has an old doghouse in his garage," said Ben. "I'll ask him if we can borrow it for dumb Debbie to sleep in."

"Why would she sleep in a doghouse?" asked Molly.

"Don't pay any attention to him," said Abby. "He's just being nasty because he doesn't like Debbie."

"A doghouse is just the place for dumb Debbie," said Ben. He walked away, taking Bessie with him.

"You better not say things like that while she's here," Abby called after him. But Ben just laughed.

"Why doesn't Ben like Debbie?" Molly asked.

"She made fun of his ears last year, and he got very mad," Abby told her.

"But Debbie said she was sorry," Molly answered. "I remember when that happened."

"Ben didn't believe her," Abby said. "He thinks she's nosy because she likes to see his boat models. And he thinks that when Debbie and I whisper together, we're whispering about him."

"Well, I hope Ben will be nice this time," said Molly. "No one is supposed to be mean or angry on Rosh Hashanah."

))

Debbie tried to be friends with Ben. She knocked politely on the door of his room and asked to see the new boat model that Abby said he was making. But Ben said no.

Later in the evening, the family gathered for a festive New Year dinner. Ben ignored Debbie, but she pretended not to notice. Abby noticed and decided not to say anything.

Debbie had brought honey cake as a present for dessert. She offered the first slice to Ben. "If you have some sweet cake, you'll have a sweet year," she said.

"I don't want any of your yucky cake," Ben told her.

Abby saw the hurt look on Debbie's face. "You're the one who's yucky!" she cried. "You've been mean to Debbie ever since she came—and now you spoiled our holiday!"

"Well, having Debbie here spoiled mine!" Ben shouted. He got up from the table and ran out of the room.

"Come on, Debbie," said Abby. "Let's go upstairs."

Debbie looked very unhappy as she followed Abby out.

"What's going on here?" asked Mom. "This is no way to behave on Rosh Hashanah."

Molly explained as well as she could.

"I'd better talk to Ben," said Dad.

Dad found Ben sitting on the back step, holding Bessie in his arms. Dad sat down next to him. "Ben," he asked quietly, "why are you so mad at Debbie?"

"I just don't like her," Ben answered. "I wish she had never come."

"You don't have to like someone if you don't want to," said Dad. "But you can be polite. You behaved badly tonight and hurt Debbie's feelings. That was wrong."

"She hurt mine," said Ben. "She made fun of my ears."

"That was last year," Dad said. "And she did apologize." Ben didn't answer.

"Tonight is the first night of Rosh Hashanah," said Dad. "On Rosh Hashanah, we all make a new start. I hope you'll try to make a new start and forgive Debbie." Dad got up and went inside.

Ben scratched Bessie under her chin and thought about what his father had said. Then he went into the house.

"I'd better get this over with," he mumbled as he climbed the stairs. He knocked on Abby's door and opened it slowly. His sister and her friend were sitting on the bed. Ben took a deep breath.

"Dad says that since it's Rosh Hashanah, I should make a fresh start and say I'm sorry. Okay—I'm sorry." Ben was about to run out of the room, but Abby stopped him.

"Ben, can Debbie please see the boat model you're making?" she asked.

Ben looked at the floor, then at the wall—anywhere but at Debbie and his sister. He knew they were looking at him. "Well . . . I guess she can . . . if she really wants to," he said finally.

Debbie followed Ben down the hall to his room. Ben opened his door and pointed wordlessly to the half-finished model propped up on the desk.

"Wow! That's a Chesapeake Bay skipjack," Debbie exclaimed.

"How did you know that?" Ben asked, surprised.

"My dad likes to make boat models," she told him. "He just finished making a skipjack. Dad had trouble setting the mast and I helped him."

"You did?" Ben was torn. He needed help with *his* mast.

"Well—you can help me if you want to," he said.

"Okay," Debbie agreed.

After a while, Abby came to look for Debbie. She heard voices coming from Ben's room. I hope they aren't fighting, she thought anxiously as she hurried down the hall.

Debbie was holding the boat model. She and Ben were laughing and talking and so busy that they never noticed Abby standing in the doorway. She tiptoed quietly away and went downstairs.

In the dining room, Mom and Dad were sitting at the table, drinking a cup of tea.

"Hi, Abby," said Mom.

"It's very quiet around here," said Dad. "And where are Ben and Debbie?"

Abby didn't say anything. She grinned at Dad, winked at Mom, and cut herself a thick slice of honey cake.

THE HUT WITH THREE WALLS

A Story for Sukkot

A gentle breeze puffed the curtains of Molly's room. It was sunny outside, but Abby was wearing shiny yellow boots and helping Molly to put on her red ones.

"Mr. Yomtov says the reeds for our sukkah roof grow in muddy places," Abby told Molly. "That's why we have to wear boots."

Abby and Molly ran downstairs just as their father opened the door for Mr. Yomtov. He was wearing boots, too. They all got into the car, and Dad drove them to Willow Lake.

"The best reeds grow here," said Mr. Yomtov as they all walked to the lakeshore. He and Dad cut the tall reeds. Molly and Abby made them into bundles and tied them with string. When they were ready to leave, Dad tied the bundles to the roof of the car.

"Look!" cried Molly as they drove up to their house. "Aunt Judy and the twins are here."

"They came to help build our sukkah," said Abby. Their twin cousins, Peter and Robert, helped carry the reed bundles into the backyard.

"The back of the house will make one wall of the sukkah," Dad explained. "We'll build the other three walls."

After an early supper, everyone gathered to build the sukkah. Abby, Ben, and Molly gave tools to whoever needed them. Peter and Robert helped hold the wooden boards in place. Mom and Aunt Judy arranged reeds on the sukkah roof so that they could see the moon and stars shine through.

By the time they were finished, it was dark and everyone was tired. "Tomorrow will be fun, too," Mom told them. "We'll decorate the inside of the sukkah. I've been saving colored paper, ribbons, and all kinds of stuff to make pretty decorations."

Dad put a big cardboard box of autumn fruits and vegetables into the sukkah. "Sukkot is like Thanksgiving," he said. "Tomorrow you can attach string to the fruits and vegetables inside and hang them up."

The children went to bed happy and excited and were up early the next morning. Abby had invited her friend Kim to help. Kim showed them how to make paper birds and animals.

Even Bessie the cat joined in the fun. She joyfully pounced on bits of colored yarn and ribbon. When Ben tossed her a walnut, she chased it all over the sukkah.

"It looks like you're all done," said Dad as he carried

a table and chairs into the sukkah. "It's time to go to the train station to pick up Grandma and Grandpa."

Before they left, Ben, Abby, and Molly took a last peek at the sukkah. Colorful fruits and vegetables dangled from ribbons tied to the roof poles. Paper chains and strings of popcorn and cranberries were looped among the reeds. Paper birds, animals, and pictures decorated the walls.

"Oh," breathed Molly. "Our sukkah is *beautiful!*"

At the train station, Dad waited in the car while Mom, Ben, Abby, and Molly stood on the train platform to look for Grandma and Grandpa.

"Uh-oh!" said Molly, wiping her cheek. "I think I felt a raindrop."

"Wow," said Ben. "Look at those black clouds! They snuck up when we weren't watching."

"Here come Grandma and Grandpa," said Mom.

"Looks like we came with the rain," Grandma told them.

"Hop in, quick," said Dad as he drove up to where they were standing. "It's starting to rain very hard."

Ben, Molly, and Abby were very quiet during the trip home. They knew the reeds would never be able to stop the rain from coming in the sukkah. The children ran to the backyard as soon as they got home.

It was very wet in the sukkah. Raindrops dripped from

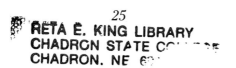

the fruits and vegetables. The paper decorations looked soggy and limp. The chairs and table were wet. In the middle of it all was Bessie, lapping water from a big puddle on the floor.

Molly began to cry. "Our beautiful sukkah is ruined!" she sobbed.

Aunt Judy arrived with the twins. They all looked very sad when they saw what the rain had done.

Mom sighed. "I think it's stopped raining," she said. "We'll try to make the best of things."

Everyone set to work. Grandpa mopped the floor. Peter and Robert wiped the table and chairs, and Ben helped Molly set the table. Grandma and Abby helped Mom get supper ready, and Dad went to get Mr. Yomtov and Abby's friend Kim. They had been invited to share in the holiday dinner.

They were so busy that no one noticed that the rain clouds had blown away. When it was almost dark, everyone sat down at the table in the sukkah to eat a festive meal. Mom lit the holiday candles and they all recited the holiday blessing.

Molly looked around. The candles filled the sukkah with soft, golden light and dancing shadows. Drops of water sparkled on the fruits and vegetables that hung from the roof.

The wind had dried most of the paper decorations.

A round, full moon was shining through the reeds of the roof. On the table, the holiday food smelled delicious.

Dad looked at the smiling faces all around him. *"Hag same'ah!* Happy holiday!" he said.

"Happy holiday!" everyone answered.

HAPPENSTANCE

A Story for Simchat Torah

"Hello, Abby," said Mr. Yomtov as he came up the walk to the Bergs' house. "I saw you from my window, sitting on your doorstep. Did you forget your key?"

Abby didn't answer, and when Mr. Yomtov came closer, he saw that she was crying. On the step next to her was a box of Simchat Torah flags. Bessie the cat was sitting on her lap.

Mr. Yomtov gave Abby his handkerchief. "If you are locked out, you and Bessie can stay at my house until your folks come home," he said.

Abby wiped her eyes. "I did forget my key," she said. "But it's worse than that. Tonight is the Simchat Torah parade in the synagogue. I'm meeting Mom, Dad, Ben, and Molly there. My Hebrew school class is in the parade, and I said I'd get apples and put them on the flags."

Abby began to cry all over again. "My teacher will be here soon to pick me up, and the flags, too. But the apples are in the house," she sobbed. "And I'm out here!"

Mr. Yomtov gave Abby time to stop crying. "Let's take a little walk," he said. "Perhaps I can think of a way to solve your problem."

Abby wasn't sure a walk would help, but crying on the step wasn't helping at all. And Mr. Yomtov's gentle face and kind smile made her feel better.

It was a lovely afternoon. They walked down the street and into a meadow near Mr. Yomtov's house. A breeze rippled through the grass and blew fluffy seed plumes from the milkweed pods. Abby stepped on something hard and bent down to see what it was.

"I found an apple!" she said.

"Where there's an apple, there must be an apple tree," said Mr. Yomtov, with a mischievous smile. He pointed to a tree with gnarled, twisty branches.

"How did you know it was here?" asked Abby.

"It was happenstance," Mr. Yomtov explained. "I found this wild apple tree in the spring, when its branches were full of blossoms."

"Now it's full of apples!" Abby was delighted. "We can gather some for my Simchat Torah flags."

"It's what I had in mind," Mr. Yomtov said, smiling. He shook the tree's lowest branches. Ripe apples tumbled to the ground.

Abby gave one to Mr. Yomtov and bit into one herself.

"Yum! They're delicious," she said. "And there's more

than enough for my flags. But how can we get them home?"

Mr. Yomtov felt around in his jacket. From one of its many pockets, he produced a neatly folded string shopping bag. "I always keep this handy," he explained. "I never know when I'll need it."

Together, he and Abby filled the bag. Mr. Yomtov carried it as they walked back to Abby's house.

Abby's teacher was just ringing the bell when Abby and Mr. Yomtov hurried across the street and up the walk.

"Mr. Gold," called Abby. "Here I am!" She explained what had happened. With Mr. Yomtov and her teacher helping, it didn't take long to put an apple atop each brightly colored flag.

Mr. Gold drove Abby and Mr. Yomtov to the synagogue, which was filled with people who had come there for Simchat Torah. After the service, the Torah scrolls were taken from the Ark and joyfully carried up, down, and around the synagogue. Abby and her class were right behind the scrolls, carrying their apple-topped flags. They were followed by more children, dancing and singing.

After the parade, Abby found the rest of her family. Molly and Ben waved their Simchat Torah flags. Mom and Dad were chatting with Mr. Yomtov.

"Mom was worried," Ben told Abby. "She said you forgot your key and that the apples you needed were in the house. How did you get them?"

Abby winked at Mr. Yomtov and he winked back. "Happenstance," she said.

THE GLASS MENORAH

A Story for Hanukkah

Mom and Molly were sitting at the kitchen table having tea and cookies one afternoon, when Ben burst in, bringing a blast of cold air.

"Today was the last rehearsal of our Hanukkah play," Ben announced as he picked up a cookie and ate it. "I'm glad I play Judah Maccabee." He raced around the kitchen, waving his arms.

"I'm the brave Maccabee leader," Ben cried. "I'll scare mean King Antiochus and his soldiers!"

"You scared Bessie," laughed Molly. "She ran upstairs."

Ben took another cookie. "What's that?" he asked, pointing to a large box on the table.

"We were just going to open it," Mom told him. "It's from Uncle Mark in Israel."

Molly undid the paper wrappings. Mom opened the box and lifted out a large object.

"Oh, it's a glass menorah!" said Molly.

"It's pretty," said Ben. "I never saw one like that."

"Here's a note from Uncle Mark," Mom said as she unfolded a piece of paper. "He says the menorah is hand-made. It's a special present for Hanukkah."

When Dad and Abby came home, each admired the beautiful glass menorah. During supper that night, everyone talked about Hanukkah and menorahs.

Ben and Abby told Molly the story of Judah Maccabee's victory and the oil that miraculously lasted for eight days.

"The Jewish people celebrated God's miracle, and that's why we celebrate," Dad said.

"And that's why we spin dreidels that have Hebrew letters on them," said Abby. "The letters stand for words that mean—"

"A great miracle happened there," finished Molly, who knew the story by heart but liked to hear it anyway.

After school the next day, Molly and Abby baked Hanukkah cookies. Dad helped Ben with his Judah Maccabee costume. Mom hung up Hanukkah decorations in the living room and put the glass menorah on the windowsill.

"Hanukkah begins tomorrow evening," she said. "When the candles are lit, people who pass by will see the lights and be able to share in the holiday."

Molly was excited because she was going to light the first candle. "Good-night, menorah," she said as she went upstairs to sleep.

The house grew quiet. Everyone was asleep, except Bessie. Light from the street lamp outside was shining on something that was sitting on the living room windowsill, and Bessie decided to investigate. She jumped up onto the windowsill for a better look and bumped into the glass menorah. It fell to the floor and broke into pieces.

Molly was the first one downstairs the next morning. She found the broken menorah and started to cry.

Abby hurried down to see what was wrong. "Bessie must have knocked it over," she said. "She's hiding under the sofa and won't come out."

"She's a bad cat," said Molly angrily. "I'm very mad at her."

"Bessie probably just wanted to look at it," sighed Abby. "She didn't mean to break it."

When Mom, Dad, and Ben came downstairs, Molly told them what had happened. "Our beautiful menorah is ruined," she said tearfully.

"Maybe not," said Dad. "The pieces are fairly large. I think we can mend it."

Before he left for work, Dad gathered up the pieces and carefully glued them together. Then he set the menorah away to dry. In the afternoon, the family went to see Ben in the Hanukkah play. He was a brave and lively Judah Maccabee, and his family clapped loudly for him at the end.

As soon as they came home, Molly, Ben, and Abby went to look at the menorah. "It's all in one piece," said Molly. "But the cracks show. It looks terrible!"

"Let's take it to Mr. Yomtov," said Abby. "He does so many special things—maybe he can do something about the menorah."

"What can he do?" said Ben. "Cracks are cracks."

When Mr. Yomtov saw the mended menorah, he shook his head sadly. "I'm not sure I can make it look better," he said. "But let's go to my workshop. We'll see."

Mr. Yomtov's workshop was a hodgepodge of all kinds of things. He put the menorah on his worktable and poked among dusty shelves and cluttered drawers. Soon paintbrushes and jars of paint were lined up in a row next to the menorah. Mr. Yomtov began to look cheerful. Humming a Hanukkah tune, he picked up a paintbrush and began to work.

Ben, Molly, and Abby watched quietly. Mr. Yomtov worked for quite a while. Finally, he put down his paintbrush.

"What do you think?" he asked.

Mr. Yomtov had painted a grapevine on the menorah. Tiny leaves, green vines, and bunches of purple grapes hid the cracks. Mr. Yomtov had even painted birds and tiny insects among the tendrils.

"It's even more beautiful than it was before!" said

Molly. The children thanked him and carried the menorah carefully home.

"Mr. Yomtov is a magician," said Mom, when she saw what he had done.

"I'll be frying a big batch of potato pancakes for Hanukkah supper tonight," said Dad. "We'll ask Mr. Yomtov to come and help us eat them."

When it was dark, Molly lit the first Hanukkah candle. After supper, they sang Hanukkah songs and played dreidel games. Molly had forgiven Bessie for breaking the glass menorah. She spun a dreidel on the floor especially for the cat to play with.

The lighted menorah sat on the windowsill. The first candle of the holiday and the helper candle used to light it glittered brightly.

Molly pointed to the menorah. "Ben played Judah Maccabee today," she said. "But Mr. Yomtov, *you* made a Hanukkah miracle for us!"

DISGUISES

A Story for Purim

"I love Purim, and Purim's almost here!" sang Molly as she and Abby walked home from school.

Abby tucked her scarf ends into her jacket. "It's very windy," she said. "If it's this windy on the day of the Purim parade, I'll have to tie my crown to my head."

"Are you going to be Queen Esther *again*?" asked Molly.

"Yes," said Abby. "I like being Queen Esther."

"I'm going to be a pirate," said Molly.

When Ben came home from school, Molly asked him what his Purim disguise would be.

"Wicked Haman—who else?" he said.

"I knew it," giggled Molly. "You're always Haman, and Abby is always Queen Esther."

"Well, I like being Haman," Ben told her. "Maybe this time I'll win the prize." Ben and Molly's Hebrew school was giving prizes for the best boy's and best girl's costumes. The two winners would lead the Purim parade.

The next day after school, Ben came into Abby's room. "Where's everybody?" he asked.

"Mom's at the library and Dad isn't home from work yet," said Abby. "And Molly is at her friend Jessy's house. They're making their costumes together."

"We should get started making *our* costumes," said Ben. "Purim's only a few days away."

"I know," Abby answered, "and I have something for you." She opened a drawer and took out something brown and fluffy. "It's an old sweater. The yarn will make a great wig and beard for your Haman disguise," she told him. "I'll help you unravel it."

Bessie had been sleeping on Abby's bed. As soon as she heard the click of the scissors, she was wide awake. Ben tossed her a scrap of yarn and said, "I wish we could put a costume on Bessie."

"Wouldn't it be fun to disguise her to look like a dog?" Abby asked.

"She'd never let us," laughed Ben. He poked at the pile of fluffy yarn thoughtfully. "But that gives me an idea." He told her what it was.

Abby giggled. "That's a great idea. Let's do it!"

On Purim eve, all the Bergs went to the synagogue to hear the rabbi read the megillah scroll that told the story of Esther. The synagogue was crowded and everyone was in a happy mood. Each time the rabbi said "Haman,"

the children shouted and twirled their groggers to drown out his name. Even the grown-ups made noise.

Ben, Molly, and Abby got up early the next day to get ready for the big Purim parade. Molly, dressed in her pirate disguise, was ready first. She waited with her parents for Ben and Abby to appear.

Ben and Abby came downstairs slowly. Queen Esther had a shiny paper crown on her fluffy woolen hair. She wore a smiling mask with pink cheeks. Her long dress was trimmed with beads and ribbon. She wore long, dangly earrings and lots of bracelets and necklaces.

Haman looked very wicked. His face was almost hidden by a woolly brown mustache, long beard, and fierce-looking eyebrows. He wore a big hat. His robe was made out of all kinds of colored cloth, and he carried a large cardboard sword.

"Abby, this is your most beautiful Esther costume ever!" said Mom.

"Ben, you're a really wicked-looking Haman," said Dad. Ben and Abby bowed.

On the way to the school, where the parade would begin, the Bergs met Mr. Yomtov. "Abby, you are a lovely queen," he said. "Ben, *you* look very scary."

When Ben and Abby arrived at their school, most of their friends were there. Everyone admired their costumes.

The school principal was to select the winning disguises. When she was ready, she stood on the school steps and held up her hands for everyone to be quiet.

"All of the costumes are wonderful," she said. "It was very hard to choose. But I have picked two winners." She pointed to Ben and Abby.

Everyone cheered and clapped as wicked Haman and Queen Esther came up the stairs to stand beside the principal. She gave them each a basket filled with candy, fruit, and hamantaschen.

"Now, tell us who you are," she said.

Ben took off his Queen Esther mask. Abby took off her Haman's beard and mustache.

"Well, this is a *real* Purim surprise," laughed the principal. Everyone cheered louder than ever.

Ben and Abby walked at the head of the Purim parade and all the children followed. Ben munched a hamantaschen. "This is my best Purim ever," he said. "We fooled everyone!"

MATZA

A Story for Passover

Abby, Ben, and Molly were staying with their grandparents while Mom and Dad went shopping for Passover. Grandma and Grandpa lived in a big city and the children loved to visit them. Today Grandpa was taking them somewhere for a special surprise.

"Grandpa, where *are* we going?" asked Molly as she, Ben, and Abby got into Grandpa's car.

"We're going to a matza factory!" Grandpa told her.

"Oh, boy! Our class took a trip to a matza factory once," said Ben. "It was a big place and the matza was made in machines."

"Our class made matza by hand last week," said Molly. "It was fun. We made dough out of flour and water. Then some of the boys threw dough balls and our teacher got really mad."

Grandpa laughed. "Well," he said, "this matza factory is very small. There are no machines. And no one will throw dough balls."

They drove for a long while. Finally Grandpa turned

onto a wide street that had elevated subway tracks running above it. He pulled up to the curb.

"We're here," he said.

Ben looked around. All he saw were brick walls and metal doors. "I don't see a matza factory," he said. "I don't even see a bakery."

"Here's the entrance," said Grandpa. He opened a door that had a sign with Hebrew letters on it and small letters in English that said PASSOVER MATZA MADE HERE.

The matza factory was a busy place. Women of all ages scurried past, tying big white aprons around their waists as they walked. A door opened and four men came out, their arms piled high with large boxes.

Molly giggled. "They look like pizza boxes," she said.

One of the men smiled at her. "That's because the matza made here is round and flat, like a pizza. And each matza is as big as a pizza. That's why we put them into these boxes."

Grandpa took the children up to a wall with a big glass window in it. They could see into a room where several women stood at a long table. A man came around with a basket. He gave each woman a small ball of dough. The women quickly rolled each ball into a thin, flat circle.

"It does look like they're making pizza," said Molly.

"Matza dough is made with flour and water, just like

pizza dough," Grandpa told her. "But pizza dough has yeast in it, to make it rise and get puffy when it's baked. Matza dough must be made without yeast."

"I know," said Ben. "Matza is like the flat bread that Jewish people ate in the desert, when Moses led them out of Egypt."

As soon as a woman finished rolling out a ball of dough, she carried it on her rolling pin to another table. Several men with little wheeled tools cut rows of tiny holes into each dough circle.

Grandpa explained that the holes made the matza easy to break into pieces after it was baked. As each man finished making holes, he draped a dough circle over a long pole on a rack above his head.

"What happens now?" asked Abby, as she watched another man carry a pole of dough circles away.

Grandpa led them to a large, warm room. "This is where the matza is baked," he told them. "The whole back wall is a giant oven that burns wood."

The oven opening looked like an arched window without any glass. Inside, they could see heaps of glowing red embers. Against another wall, logs were stacked as high as the ceiling.

The baker took a pole of dough circles, slid it into the oven, and flipped the circles onto the oven floor.

"The baker has to be very careful," Grandpa said.

"Matza bakes very quickly. If the circles are left in the oven too long, they burn."

It took less than a minute for the matza to bake. The baker used a big wooden paddle to take them out of the oven. He slid the freshly baked matza into a wire basket to cool.

"Even the matza paddle looks like a pizza paddle," said Molly.

The baker laughed. "The pizza maker does use the same kind of paddle. And a pizza oven is like a matza oven, but it doesn't usually burn wood." He walked over to a basket of broken matza and gave them each a piece to eat. Before they left, Grandpa bought two boxes of the special handmade matzot.

The next morning, they all drove to the Bergs' house. Passover would begin at sunset. Mom and Dad were delighted with Grandpa's present of the handmade matzot.

Everyone helped to set the table for the Passover seder. Abby wrapped three matzot in an embroidered cloth and put them on a platter in front of her father's place at the table. Ben got the seder plate ready. Molly put a haggadah book at each person's place.

When the sun set it was time for the seder to begin. Everyone took a turn reading from the haggadah, which told the story of Passover. Then Dad unwrapped the matzot and split the middle one in half.

He broke one of the halves into small pieces and gave each person some to eat. He wrapped the other half in a napkin and held it up. "This is the afikoman," he said. "I'll hide it when no one is watching, and whoever finds it gets a prize."

When dinner was over, Molly, Ben, and Abby searched for the afikoman. They couldn't find it anywhere. They went into the living room and sat down on the sofa to think.

"We looked and looked," said Abby. "Where could it be?"

Ben didn't answer. He was watching Bessie the cat. She was sitting on top of an armchair, swatting at a bit of cloth that was hanging down behind a picture frame.

"Bessie, what are you up to now?" Ben said. He reached behind the picture.

"It's the afikoman!" he said. "Bessie found it." He picked up the cat and carried her into the dining room.

Molly gave her father the afikoman. He gave everyone some to eat, to end the seder.

"Bessie wins the prize," laughed Dad. "We'll buy her a nice catnip mouse. What do you think of that, Bessie?"

The cat seemed to understand. She closed her eyes and purred.

TWO BIRTHDAYS

A Story for Shavuot

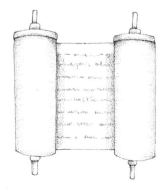

Molly opened her window and breathed the sweet spring air.

"Today is really special," she told Bessie. The cat was sitting on Molly's bed in a patch of sunshine.

"It's a day of two birthdays, Bessie. It's my birthday and it's Shavuot—the Jewish people's birthday."

Molly fastened the buttons on her favorite dress. "I'm going to have a special part in Shavuot services at the synagogue today, because I'll be going to Hebrew school in the fall."

Bessie blinked her eyes and twitched her ears, as if she understood what Molly was saying.

When Molly came downstairs, Mom, Dad, Ben, and Abby told her how pretty she looked. But they didn't say anything about her birthday.

"Here's Mr. Yomtov," said Mom as the doorbell rang. Mr. Yomtov was going to the synagogue with them. He didn't say anything about Molly's birthday, either. Molly was surprised, but she didn't have time to think about it. They were meeting Grandma and Grandpa, Aunt Judy, and the twins, and they had to hurry or they'd be late.

The synagogue was decorated inside with spring flowers, in remembrance of the flowers that grew on Mount Sinai when Moses received the Ten Commandments from God. During the service, the rabbi read the Bible story of Ruth and she recited the Ten Commandments.

The children's service was beautiful. The rabbi asked the children who were in Hebrew school to stand before the Ark. They helped the cantor sing part of the service and they recited Torah prayers. Then it was Molly's turn. She sang *"ein kelohenu"*—"There is none like our God."

When the services were over, Molly's family told her now nicely she had sung—but not a word about her birthday!

I guess they all forgot, Molly thought sadly as they walked home. The Jewish people's birthday is important, but my birthday is important, too.

It seemed to Molly that it was taking a long time to get home. Everyone was busy talking. No one seemed to notice that Molly was very quiet.

When they arrived at the house, Mom told Molly to go up and wash her hands. "We'll be eating lunch in a minute," she said.

Molly was too unhappy to be hungry. She washed her hands slowly and took her time coming down the stairs.

"Happy birthday, dear Molly!"

Everyone was in the dining room, and they clapped

and sang as Molly walked in. Even Mr. Yomtov was there.

For a moment, Molly couldn't say anything. On the table were her favorite Shavuot foods—cheese blintzes, sour cream, and a big dish of strawberries. A pile of birthday presents was stacked on her chair.

Best of all was a beautiful birthday cake that said, "Happy Birthday, Molly, on this Special Shavuot." The cake was decorated with icing roses and a little candy Torah scroll.

"Oh," said Molly happily. "I thought everyone had forgotten my birthday."

"This year, your birthday is special," Dad said. "So we planned a special surprise."

"Mr. Yomtov helped," said Abby. "He rushed here after the services and set everything out, to be ready when we came home."

"So *that's* why we walked so slowly," Molly laughed.

Everyone smiled at Molly, and she smiled back. Grandma lit the seven candles on Molly's cake. Molly made a wish, took a deep breath, and blew them all out in one puff.

Grandpa gave Molly the little candy Torah scroll. "When you go to Hebrew school, you will learn all about Torah," he said. "I hope your studies will be as sweet as candy!"

Day and Night

According to the Jewish calendar, a new day begins at sunset. This is because it says in the Bible: "... and God divided the light from the darkness. And God called the light Day and the darkness He called Night. And there was evening and there was morning, one day."

In the Jewish religion, evening comes first, and then morning. Both are part of the same day. This is why the Jewish Sabbath begins at sunset on Friday and ends at sunset on Saturday. It is why all dates on the Jewish calendar, including the holidays, begin on the evening before the first full day.

Glossary

afikoman: A Greek word for dessert. The afikoman is eaten after dinner to end the Passover seder.

Ark: A cabinet in which the Torah scrolls are kept.

blintzes: Pancakes rolled up and stuffed with cheese, potatoes, or fruit.

cantor: One who sings or chants, to lead the Jewish congregation in prayer.

challah: A festive bread, usually braided, that is eaten on the Sabbath and other Jewish holidays.

dreidel: A four-sided top that children and adults use to play games with during Hanukkah.

haggadah: A book containing the seder service that is recited during the Passover seder.

Haman: A wicked man who plotted to kill the Jews of Persia long ago.

hamantaschen: Small triangular cookies filled with jam that are eaten during Purim. The shape is supposed to resemble a hat worn by Haman.

Hanukkah: The Festival of Dedication. It is also called the Festival of Lights.

kiddush: A blessing recited before Sabbath and holiday meals, usually with wine.

Judah Maccabee: A great hero and leader of the Jewish people.

matza (plural, matzot): Unleavened bread made with flour and water and eaten during Passover.

megillah: A scroll. It usually refers to the Scroll of Esther, the Biblical Book of Esther.

menorah: A branched candlestick. The Hanukkah menorah has nine branches: eight candles for each day the oil lasted in the Biblical story of Judah Maccabee and a "helper" candle used to light them.

Moses: A great leader of the Jewish people. He led them out of slavery in Egypt long ago.

Mount Sinai: A mountain in the Sinai Desert, where long ago God gave the Ten Commandments to Moses.

Passover: The Festival of Unleavened Bread. It is also called the Festival of Freedom.

Purim: The Festival of Esther, also known as the Festival of Lots.

Queen Esther: A Jewish woman honored because she saved her people, the Jews of Persia, from death.

rabbi: A master or teacher. He or she may also be the spiritual leader of a Jewish community.

Rosh Hashanah: The Jewish New Year.

Sabbath: Saturday—the seventh day of the week. The observance of a day of rest and peace—the most important Jewish holiday.

scroll: A roll of parchment, or paper. Also, the writing on such a roll.

seder: The service conducted at the meal eaten on Passover eve.

Shavuot: The Feast of Weeks. It is also called Pentecost, because it arrives fifty days after the first day of Passover.

Simchat Torah: The festive day at the end of Sukkot, when the yearly cycle of Torah readings is completed and begins again.

Sukkot: The Festival of Tabernacles. It is also called the Festival of Booths and the Festival of Harvest.

Ten Commandments: The ten laws that God gave to Moses on Mount Sinai.

Torah (Scrolls of the Law): They are the first five books of the Bible: Genesis, Exodus, Leviticus, Numbers, and Deuteronomy. "Torah" also means all Jewish learning and tradition.

Torah Scrolls: The first five books of the Bible, written on a parchment scroll.